W9-AEH-534

Wildlife Rescue

Wildlife Rescue

The Work of Dr. Kathleen Ramsay

by Jennifer Owings Dewey

photographs by Don MacCarter

BOYDS MILLS PRESS

Acknowledgments

⌒

I would like to thank Don MacCarter for his complete dedication to this book and for his willingness to take pictures no matter what day of the week or hour of the day. Not only did he help in every way possible, he made the whole thing much more fun than it would have been otherwise. — J.O.D.

I wish to thank the New Mexico Department of Game and Fish for supporting the time and energy I spent on this project. Without the department's stamp of approval I would never have been able to participate. — D.M.

Photographs by Jennifer Owings Dewey: Pages 1, 12, 17 top, 18 bottom, 20 top and bottom, 22 top, 23, 24 middle left, 26 bottom, 29 bottom, 37 top, 38 top, 39 bottom, 42 bottom, 45, 48 bottom, 53, 54, 55. All other photographs taken by Don MacCarter.

Published by Caroline House
Boyds Mills Press, Inc.
A Highlights Company
815 Church Street
Honesdale, Pennsylvania 18431
Printed in Mexico

Publisher Cataloging-in-Publication Data
Dewey, Jennifer Owings.
    Wildlife rescue : the work of Dr. Kathleen Ramsay / by Jennifer Owings Dewey;
photographs by Don MacCarter.
— 1st ed.
[64] p. : col. photo. ; cm.
Summary : How the Wildlife Center, based in Española, New Mexico, and headed by
Dr. Kathleen Ramsay, nurtures sick and injured animals back to health.
ISBN 1-56397-045-7
1. Wildlife rescue – New Mexico – Española. 2. Wildlife Center (veterinary hospital).
3. Ramsay, Kathleen – Juvenile literature. [1. Wildlife rescue. 2. Ramsay, Kathleen.]
I. MacCarter, Don, photographer. II. Title.
639.95 – dc20   1994   CIP

Library of Congress Catalog Card Number 93-71478

First edition, 1994
Book designed by Jeanne Abboud
The text of this book is set in 13-point Clearface.
Distributed by St. Martin's Press

10 9 8 7 6 5 4 3 2

For my grandson, Kyle
— J.O.D.

For my dad,
and in memory of my mother
— D.M.

Contents

Wally and Theo

~

INTRODUCTION

It was early spring in Gila, New Mexico, a mountainous region of piñon pine forest and deep, sandy arroyos. The sun was out but the air was cold. A woman and her two young daughters, aged ten and fourteen, decided to take an afternoon walk. The family dog went with them. They walked up an arroyo with a narrow watercourse down the middle. Sunlit muddy pools dotted the streamside.

The dog ran forward, splashing in the water and mud. A few hundred

yards ahead of the others he paused and raised his head. He sniffed the air, sensing another animal near. Just then a splash disturbed the surface of a pool. The dog jumped and landed feetfirst in the water, anticipating a joyful encounter with whatever hid there.

Seventy pounds of enraged female beaver attacked the dog at the moment his paws touched bottom. The beaver sank her huge front teeth into the dog's soft flesh. Blood flowed into her mouth. The dog struggled desperately to free himself from the beaver's tearing bite. He howled with pain.

The woman and the two girls raced up the arroyo, their feet sinking into loose, yielding sand. They found the dog at the edge of the water, bleeding and shaking, seemingly in shock. One of the girls ran to him, crying. Suddenly the beaver spun around to attack the child.

The mother couldn't believe her eyes. No beaver had ever been seen on their property, and none were known to live nearby. Yet a big, angry beaver had just attacked and nearly killed their dog and was now turning on her daughter.

The woman picked up a heavy stick and approached the water. The beaver snarled with fury. The woman struck the beaver twice on the head with the stick. Each blow made a dry thudding sound. The second one crushed the beaver's skull and killed her.

A neighbor, hearing the commotion, came running. He stared at the dead beaver, the bleeding dog, the woman with the stick, and the two astonished girls.

"What happened? Are you okay?" the man asked, grabbing the woman's arm.

"Yes, I think we're fine," the woman replied. "The beaver attacked our dog." Then, a moment later, she gasped, "Look! There's a baby coming...."

The man and the woman and both children watched in amazement as a minute, wet beaver baby nose began to slide out of the dead mother's back end.

In a single gesture the man pulled a knife from his coat and bent over the fallen beaver. He slit her belly from chest to tail. Two beaver kits fell out on the ground, each about the size of a navel orange. They were wet with blood and fluids from their mother's womb.

"Are they dead?" one of the girls asked, certain that they were.

"Looks to me like they're breathing," the man answered. "I think they're alive."

"That explains why she attacked," the woman said.

The man cut the cords and lifted the kits out of the mud. They were breathing. The woman took one in her hands. The man took the other. Bubbles appeared around each miniature muzzle, a sure sign that air was passing in and out. The kits were breathing on their own.

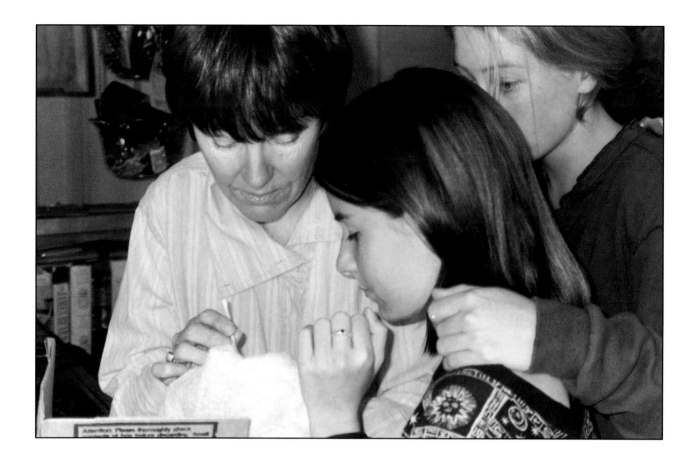

Momentarily, everyone turned their attention to the dog, who was injured, but not fatally.

Back in her warm kitchen, the woman cleaned the beavers' nasal passages with cotton swabs while the girls watched. She blew air into their lungs and gently thumped their tiny chests. Each daughter held a beaver and rubbed it dry with a cloth. The kits wriggled and squirmed. They squeaked and mewed. Once dry, their fur was a vivid, glossy brown, as soft as moss.

When she was quite sure they were going to live, the woman called the local game and fish officer. She told how she had killed the beaver mother with a stick and helped deliver two live young. The officer said he would come and collect the kits.

Arrangements were made to transport the beaver kits to a facility in Española, New Mexico, called the Wildlife Center. The founder of the center and its chief doctor, Kathleen Ramsay, was known for accepting challenges, especially where baby animals were concerned. As a veterinarian she had the skills to care for the kits medically. As a rehabilitator she could provide them with a safe environment in which to grow.

The officer put the beaver kits, safely tucked into the bottom of a cardboard box lined with rags, onto an airplane so they could be flown to Albuquerque. A volunteer from the center met the plane and drove the kits seventy miles north to a quiet agricultural valley, home of the Wildlife Center.

The airplane had carried the kits to a place far from their native stream. They would never know that their survival had been a miraculous fluke. Instead of dying by inches inside their mother's body, they were on their way into the future. And they had a chance for a good beaver life.

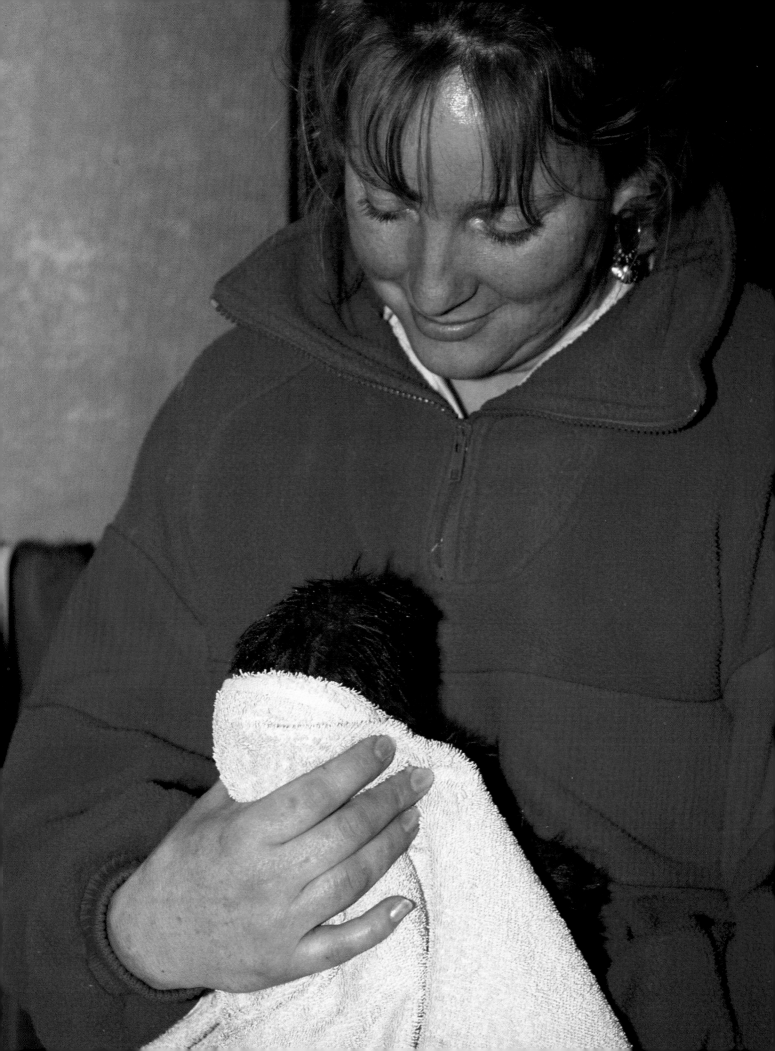

The Wildlife Center

PART ONE

Minutes after arriving at the Wildlife Center, the beaver kits are lifted from their box. They are shivering, sopping wet from their own droppings. Lynne, Dr. Ramsay's number one assistant, wraps them in a fresh towel and holds them close. She peers into one furry visage and then the other, as if to read their thoughts. "I'll bet you're hungry," she whispers.

But for their trembling limbs the beavers might be sleeping. Their

eyes are dull and half-shut. Lynne knows they have gone too long without nourishment. By now their mother's teats would have provided them with quantities of rich, warm milk.

Lynne, who has been with Dr. Ramsay for six years, handles the kits with measured, methodical care. She has endless patience for soothing wild creatures stricken with fear in new surroundings or weakened by hunger and injury. Lynne and Dr. Ramsay understand each other. Often they work side by side, pinning a broken wing bone or stitching a wound. They work under great stress and to the point of exhaustion. Lynne's composure and self-possession

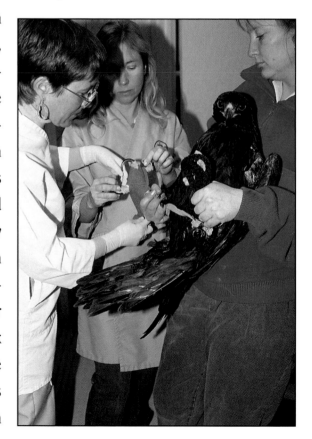

Lynne holds a golden eagle while Dr. Ramsay attends to a wound.

16 ~

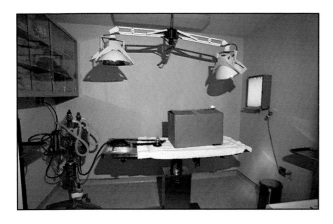

are the perfect complement to Kathleen's high-energy intensity.

The operating room, with X-ray and anesthesia equipment.

Lynne carries the beavers into the examining room, where white lights reflect off stainless steel equipment. A piece of blue and gray X-ray machinery stands in one corner. Separated from the exam room by a half-wall made of glass is a small, compact operating room with cone-shaped lights overhead and a shiny operating table. A strange-looking device with hoses attached, which delivers anesthesia, stands next to the table.

Lynne holds a quivering fur-ball of dehydrated baby beaver so Kathleen can insert a yellow tube down its throat and into its stomach. The beaver squeals in protest and empties the contents of its bladder. Not much comes out. Once a stream of fluid begins flowing through the tube and into its stomach, the kit settles down. The fluid is a mixture of water, glucose, and minerals. Kathleen uses this procedure, called "tubing," on all dehydrated animals when they first arrive.

The infusion of life-restoring liquid takes effect quickly. The beaver's beady eyes brighten. It begins a series of surprisingly loud squeaks. Kathleen watches and laughs. She takes the animal from Lynne and holds it upside down. She looks closely at its back end. "A male," she declares, as if personally responsible for this fact. "We need a name, Lynne."

A flight cage at the Wildlife Center allows some freedom for recuperating birds.

The second beaver kit has waited its turn, bound up in a towel on a countertop. This one turns out to be a male as well. The names Wally and Theo are chosen. (Lynne picks one, Kathleen the other.) The names are recorded on charts, along with information about the kits' physical conditions, their place of birth, the date and time of their arrival, and the reason for their coming.

In the waiting room at the clinic.

"We'll need an incubator for these two," Kathleen tells Lynne. "At least for twenty-four hours."

Lynne swaddles the two kits and goes off to find an unoccupied incubator.

Kathleen is repeatedly interrupted while treating the beavers. The receptionist, a soft-spoken dark-eyed woman named Anita, comes in to say three seriously ill baby raccoons are on the way. They are coming from the animal shelter in Santa Fe, twenty miles south. A person calls about a freshly hatched woodpecker, "the size of a cherry tomato," that has apparently fallen from its nest. The caller wants to know how to feed it.

Another caller asks about moving a swallow's nest filled to the brim with baby swallows. Construction is going on at the caller's house and the nest is in the way.

The Department of Game and Fish in Taos, a town to the north, calls to say some hikers have found an abandoned fawn. The ranger thinks the fawn has a broken leg and wants to bring it in.

Kathleen fires responses over her shoulder. She seems to relish activity and to enjoy a certain level of chaos. She wonders out loud what ails the

three raccoons, thinking it might be distemper. She answers the woodpecker call herself. "See if you can find the nest and put the baby back," she advises.

Workers at the clinic help care for the "patients."

The day the beaver kits come, there is a constant flow of animal patients through the examining room. Kathleen treats a great horned

owl with a bullet hole in its head. She checks a Cooper's hawk recovering from a leg fracture. Two golden eagles have sores on their feet that need bandaging. A burrowing owl loses a toe to amputation. Lynne brings the birds in, their heads covered with towels. When Kathleen is finished, Lynne takes the birds away. To protect herself from talons and beaks, Lynne wears heavy leather gloves, although most of the bird patients are docile.

Lynne holds a golden eagle with injured wings.

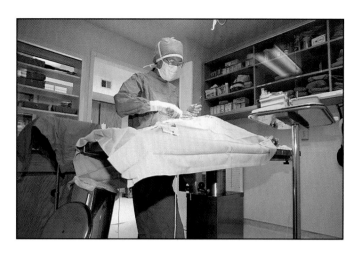

Kathleen at work in the operating room.

Kathleen gently pulls wrappings from partially healed wounds and probes infected tissue with razor-sharp blades. She uses a slender curved needle, and thread that is nearly invisible, to sew the ragged edges of torn flesh together.

Every wound gets a slathering of salve, called *Enserada,* applied with Kathleen's fingers. The salve is a special kind blended by a *curandera,* an elderly Hispanic woman in the mountains who knows cures. It is dark yellow and smells piney. Pine pitch and beeswax are the main ingredients. Kathleen admits she does not know everything that is in the salve. She does know it works.

Little of Kathleen's energy is wasted. She decides not to stop for lunch but instead downs a giant-sized cola. She uses a direct, no-nonsense approach with the people around her and with callers. Her voice is strong and commanding, sometimes sharp. Kathleen is in love with her work. She calls it "a way of life, not a job."

The injured leg of a great horned owl, before and after Enserada *treatment.*

For seven years Kathleen Ramsay's passion has been the rescue and rehabilitation of wild animals. Raptors, especially eagles, are her main

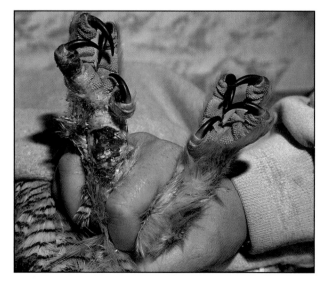

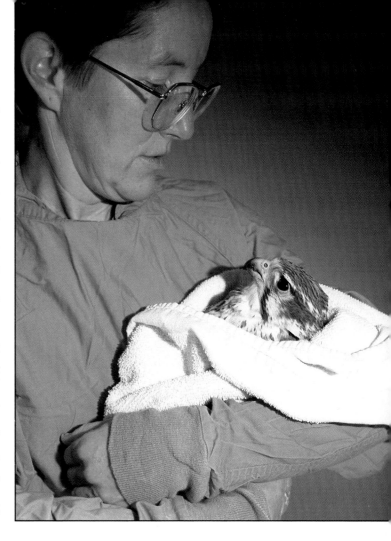

interest, but she treats anything that comes in the door.

As a young veterinary student in Colorado, Kathleen was presented one day with a golden eagle dangling its legs in a steel trap. The eagle was near death. Kathleen saw a light in the bird's amazing eyes. She has never forgotten what she glimpsed there.

Kathleen nursed the golden eagle back to health by a slow and arduous process of applying ointments and bandages and then waiting. The memory of the eagle's ordeal has become a driving force in Kathleen. She knows that man-made fences, power lines, guns, and automobiles do not mix with wildness.

Rehabilitators and veterinarians around the country are aware of Kathleen's work. Her surgery on birds is innovative and groundbreaking. Birds are brought from as close as the Sangre de Cristo Mountains near Santa Fe and from as far away as Alaska. Kathleen ignores rules and takes risks. In her mind, most efforts are worth making, and every chance is worth taking if it means restoring a wild creature to its natural habitat.

Kathleen holds a prairie falcon after surgery.

Kathleen works to repair the prairie falcon's wing.

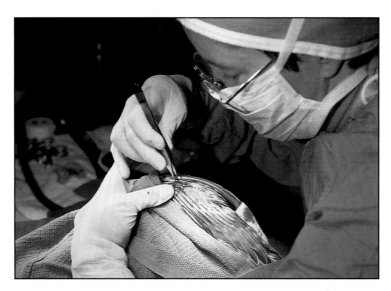

With deft fingers and gentle precision, Kathleen ministers to broken wing bones, fractured legs, and open sores. Under her hands, sinew snaps, tendons are

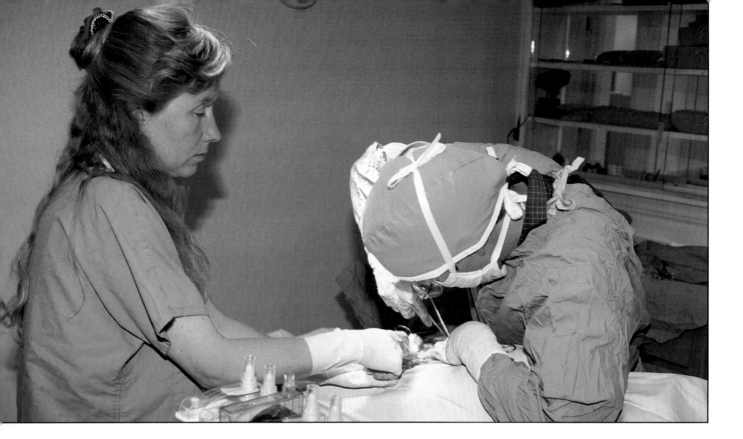

A clinic volunteer assists Dr. Ramsay.

severed, and blood rushes. The surgeon's blade seems to brutalize tender flesh, causing more trauma than the original injury. But this is deceptive. Flesh is tenacious, and Kathleen is stubborn. When she drills a steel pin into a bird's bone, the procedure looks doomed. But it works. Shattered bones come together again, and wings become usable once more.

The golden eagle is put into "intensive care."

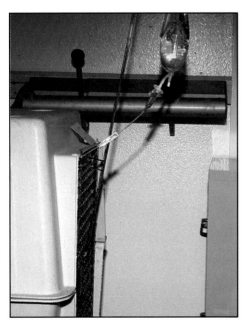

Anita comes into the examining room with more news. A golden eagle has been delivered by Game and Fish. The eagle is nearly comatose. Kathleen kneels on the floor and stares into the box where the eagle lies. Tears come to her eyes.

The eagle's veins and tissues are saturated with lead, a result of its eating wild ducks riddled with lead shot. The eagle convulses several times during Kathleen's examination. A mournful cry spills from the bird's throat, an eerie, unearthly sound. Kathleen's face constricts with anger and sympathy. She rushes Lynne, giving rapid instructions, trying not to let her emotions get in the way of what she must do.

The eagle, a female, goes into "intensive care," a carrying kennel with towels for a mattress. An intravenous device is set up. A needle is pressed into the eagle's flesh. The needle is connected to a tube attached to a plain plastic bag. Inside the bag is a clear fluid containing calcium disodium versenate, an expensive drug that will act to bind with the lead so the bird's body can dispose of it.

One vial of the medicine costs seventy dollars. The eagle will require one a day for many weeks, if she makes it. The question is, How long can the eagle survive, with lead in every cell, for the medicine to take full effect?

The eagle lies on her stomach in confinement, her head turned to one side, as if prostrate with grief. Her cries are low and drawn out. They can be heard throughout the center's small building.

Kathleen reluctantly turns her attention from the eagle. The person who called about the swallow's nest calls back. The nest has been safely moved, and the caller wants Kathleen to know.

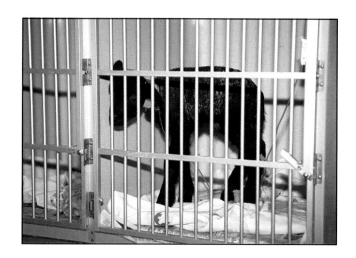

"Patients" at the clinic are given all sorts of environments in which to recuperate.

There is a quiet moment in the examining room. Kathleen leans tiredly against the counter and rubs her eyes. Then the raccoons come in.

All three have distemper. One is much sicker than the other two. They are furious and snarling, difficult to handle. Kathleen and Lynne wear leather gloves.

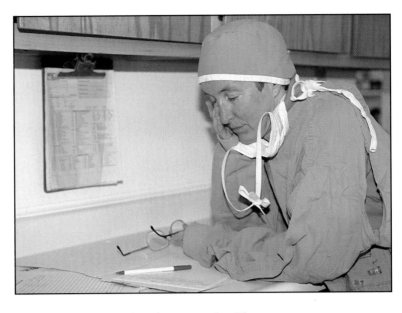

Kathleen determines the age of the raccoons by their teeth. She thinks they are two weeks old and from the same litter. "People don't realize raccoons get dog and cat diseases," she says. "They take orphan coons to the shelter, and the next thing you know the babies are sick."

The little creatures act out their fright. Their spindly arms and legs

fly. Kathleen gives them shots before offering fluids and gobs of baby-food veal on the end of a tongue depressor. Despite their anger and fear, they accept the food.

Each raccoon gets a private cage with a towel over the front for privacy. Seeing human beings coming and going can be as stressful for wild animals as recovering from a deadly virus.

It is late in the day when the fawn comes in. There is

One of the baby raccoons arriving at the clinic.

A golden eagle gets a foot soak.

no broken leg. The fawn, a female, is in perfect condition. Every leg is straight and true.

The hikers saw the fawn on the ground and mistakenly believed she had been abandoned by her mother. Kathleen takes time out to explain to the hikers, a young man and woman, about fawns. "A doe will leave her fawn concealed in grass, camouflaged, usually under a tree in dappled shade. Fawns this young have no odor other animals can detect. This one is only four or five days old. The doe knows her own fawn. She comes back after she grazes for a while."

The hikers listen. They look sad and distressed.

"We will take care of the fawn. Give me your telephone number, and I'll call you when she is released."

The hikers give some money to Anita for the care and feeding of the fawn. Then they leave.

The sun goes down behind a range of blue mountains in the west. It is late before the last staff member and volun-

The deer fawn is in perfect health.

teer drive out of the parking lot and head for home. Kathleen has a husband and a three-year-old son, and yet she keeps longer hours than anyone else. Before closing for the night, she checks the golden eagle to make sure the needle is placed securely and the solution is flowing properly.

It is close to ten o'clock when the beaver kits settle down and fall asleep. They snuggle next to each other in an incubator, the same kind used for human babies. Under them is a bedding of bright blue terry cloth beach towel, folded twice.

Earlier in the day the kits accepted nursing bottles filled with a rich mixture of goat's milk and whipping cream. At first they rejected the bottles because the rubber nipple tasted nothing like a mother beaver's teat. A few dribbles of milk on their noses changed their minds. Hunger got the better of them.

Before dawn the golden eagle cries for the final time. Her heart stops; her bloodstream is too burdened by lead for the medicine to help. Kathleen is usually the first to arrive in the morning, and no doubt she will go directly to the eagle before doing anything else. The beautiful bird's passing will be mourned.

Baby Season

PART TWO

The Wildlife Center staff and volunteers call it "baby season," that time in the spring when a bewildering assortment of animal babies floods the center. The resident population goes out of control, with every cage, incubator, carrying kennel, crate, and box occupied. There is no room at the inn.

Warm April days and nights without freezing temperatures launch spring migration. Flocks of birds return to New Mexico from southern regions where they have spent the winter. The season of court-

An orphaned bear cub arrives at the clinic.

ship and mating begins. Birds and other animals display their best features before the opposite sex of their species. Old bonds are reconfirmed, pairs join forces, mates are chosen for the first time.

Hummingbirds weave spider silk, moss, and delicate threadlike twigs into compact little nests. Owls gather grasses, sticks, leaves, deer hair, and soil for their nests. With materials similar to those the owls use, hawks build nests on rock ledges, or high in the cotton-woods along ditchbanks and arroyos. Some, like the marsh hawk, nest on the ground.

Flocks of mountain bluebirds, their wings flashing in the sun, swirl out of the prairie sage and head for the foothills, where they will nest in colonies and raise large numbers of young.

Ravens and magpies make messy constructions of dead sticks that look ready to fall down. The male and female of these species will stay together for several generations of bird-rearing.

Flickers drill into tree trunks or people's houses. They use their bills to hollow chambers roomy enough for their bulky offspring. The sound of their drilling is loud on a spring morning.

Mammal pairs are busy. Female coyotes dig new dens, the aroma of turned earth raw in their noses. Raccoons, skunks, and all kinds of rodents find shelter in hidden-away places where it is safe to give birth. Up in the mountains, amid pine trees and boulders, marmots and bobcats use dead grass to line their burrows and dens, making a soft bedding for their litters.

Usually everything goes well and animal babies thrive in their natural homes, their parents looking after them. But, sadly, there are times when things go wrong.

A pregnant elk is hit by a car on a remote mountain road. As she lies dying on the pavement, she goes into labor and a baby is born. The driver brings the newborn to the center.

A hiker finds a feathery pile of great horned owlets on the ground, their nest blown apart in a storm. The hiker knows the parent birds will feed their young, even with the nest destroyed. But a coyote is certain to find them first. So the hiker brings them in.

A doe is shot by a poacher. New Mexico has many poachers. The shooter does not realize the "kill" has a fawn. Three days after the doe is dragged away, the fawn is discovered in the woods, staggering and near death. It is brought to the center.

A baby badger is brought in.

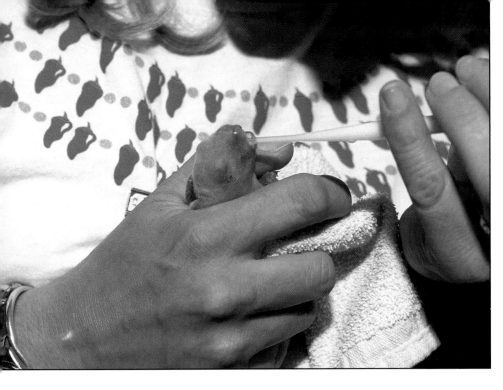

A baby rabbit is given round-the-clock feedings; its mother was killed by a car.

The story of the beaver kits is especially violent, yet most tales of orphaned animals include death and destruction. Kathleen and her staff know that the babies, who are the innocent victims of accidents, natural disasters, and catastrophic encounters with human beings, represent hope for the future of their species.

A week after coming to the center, the beaver kits have outgrown their incubator. They are living in an outdoor cage. Each weighs about two pounds and is covered with a thick coat of reddish-brown hair. Their wide, flat tails have a rough texture. Long claws on front and hind feet are useful for scratching. A big basin of water is put into their cage, a swimming hole for their water games.

Each kit gets a bottle six times every twenty-four hours. Staff people alternate taking the kits home for night feedings. A diet of goat's milk and cream has been expanded so that now, at one week, the kits also get baby-food mixed fruit and vegetables. Cathy, one of Dr. Ramsay's young assistants, usually has feeding duty in the daylight hours.

Seated on a chair in a small sunny room, Cathy holds a beaver kit on her lap. He tugs at the nipple, his front paws wrapped around the neck of the bottle as if the delicious meal might be snatched away. Yellowish liquid squirts out the sides of his mouth and dribbles on his chest. He seems not to notice. Eating is what matters.

The second beaver is on the floor waiting his turn, crawling around the legs of furniture. Both of the kits are thriving. They look like furry cantaloupes with tails and cannot be told apart.

Following every meal the kits are returned to their cage, where they have access to their swimming pool. Beavers of any size or age will not normally urinate or defecate unless they are in water.

Young beavers in the wild live in nuclear families with parents that mate for life. Wally and Theo will have a different sort of life. When human hands plucked them from their mother's body, their destiny was changed forever.

A newborn animal, with a fuzzy, unfocused vision, hears "mom" but cannot see her. The baby's vision clears when it is four or five days of age. The first moving object the baby sees becomes "mother." A baby usually sees its own

true mother. Imprinting takes place in the baby's brain. A bond is formed—a connection that can never be undone.

If the newborn happens to be a beaver kit, and the first fuzzy image it sees when it opens its eyes is a human being, then the human becomes "mother." Wally and Theo smelled and saw humans from the instant of their birth and will always feel comfortable around people and trust them.

Imprinting cannot be avoided in bottle-fed baby animals. These

infants must be held, fed, and given affection — all by human hands.

The elk calf and the deer fawns get bottles of goat's milk, just like the beaver kits. When they are ready to chew, they receive a commercial product called Calf Manna. Calf Manna comes in pellet form.

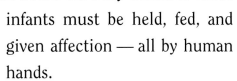

The kits take to water easily.

Lynne feeds an elk calf.

The pellets consist of milk products and grains. Like goat's milk, Calf Manna is high in protein and fat.

Lynne feeds the deer fawns and the elk calf. They come to recognize her as "mother" and run to her when she enters their enclosure. Nudging and bumping with soft heads and wet muzzles, they seem to say "Feed me!"

Together with one husband, five dogs, four cats, eight rabbits, and three birds, Lynne has two small sons at home. The younger is still nursing during the time Lynne is caring for the deer fawns. Volunteers wonder if the fawns smell "mother's milk" when Lynne approaches.

The fawn thinks Lynne is its "mother."

"No," Lynne explains. "They are used to me feeding them every day. They cannot smell my milk, though they could have smelled their own mother's milk."

The fawns grow quickly. In two weeks they are able to munch on Calf Manna, graze on the center lawn, and eat alfalfa hay. It will be six to twelve weeks before they lose their spots. Yet with their delicate, sensitive ears and flickering tails, they are beginning to resemble grown-up deer.

Dr. Ramsay feeds two baby bobcats.

Baby season peaks in May and June. Kathleen's time is consumed with medical emergencies and surgeries. Her staff members act as orderlies and nurses, tending the patients while they mend.

Lynne watches over the raptors and takes care of the mammals. Debbie is the amphibian and reptile expert. She is comfortable with snakes, lizards, frogs, and turtles. She understands their hungers and habits. Diane is the songbird person.

In baby season, most of Diane's charges are songbird nestlings. They are orphans, blind and helpless, with miniature hearts fluttering behind paper-thin breasts.

Diane gives the tiniest nestlings a high-protein diet of mashed insects, baby-food meat, and chopped eggs. Hummingbird babies get a commercially made nectar loaded with vitamins. As birds grow, Diane introduces them to seed mixtures. Often the seeds are blended with water to make a kind of soup.

A baby finch recovers from a broken wing.

Songbird nestlings eat willingly and often. Frequency tapers off as they get older. Diane ferries nestlings home every evening because

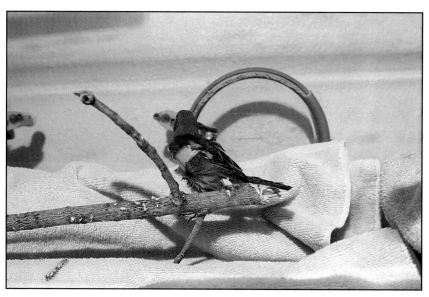

they eat until sunset. Fortunately for Diane and her husband, baby birds sleep through the night. At sunrise they awaken, their delicate see-through beaks open and voices shrill. The every-half-hour feeding program starts anew.

The center's warmest room is given over to the sickest and youngest. Shoelace-sized garter-snake young stay in a terrarium. A baby jackrabbit hides in the bottom of a cardboard box, shredded newspaper draped around its ears. Crow nestlings curl up in a teacup-shaped wad on a towel in a clear plastic container.

Imprinting is always a concern. Imprinting jeopardizes an animal's chances of being free. An imprinted animal is a danger to itself because it is not self-reliant, as wild animals are. Also, it does not know cruelty or mistreatment from humans, only kind and gentle handling.

Full-time resident birds at the center — raptors injured beyond total recovery — are pressed into service during baby season. Called "non-releasables," some are imprints themselves. These birds become surrogate or adoptive parents to babies of the same species. Raptor nestlings can be raised by another raptor, where mammal babies must be fed by humans.

Oscar, a non-releasable great horned owl, raises as many as eighteen owlets in a season. The fact that Oscar is male doesn't matter. The owlets in his charge screech with such hungry persistence that Oscar gives in. He drops portions of minced mouse down their throats. He does his job grudgingly, but he does it.

Oscar, the surrogate parent, raises as many as eighteen owlets a year.

When no imprints or non-releasables are available, a "skin" is often used. The feathery pelt of a dead bird, wrapped around someone's hand, becomes a puppet-parent. Nestlings are fooled. They accept mice bits from the impostor. They miss out on physical contact with another bird, but at least they eat.

Oscar's foster "children" thrive under his care and eventually go free.

There are no imprinting worries with songbirds. These birds have such fast metabolisms and short childhoods that they are well on their way to independence in a few short weeks.

Lynne has helped train volunteers to assist her in teaching releasables about hunting and fending for themselves in the wild. When raptor nestlings grow to fledglings, they are old enough to be

placed in special cages with movable sheet-metal sides. No visitors are allowed. Live rats and mice are tossed in with the young birds. No other food is offered. The rodent prey is eventually hunted down and killed. Non-imprinted birds possess a powerful instinct for hunting. Their skills need only be refined.

The weight, caloric intake, and general health of the captive animals are monitored daily. A log is kept, marking who ate what and when. Many of the animals are fed dead rats, mice, or chicken parts. Road kills are a source of food for the center. Volunteers are often called out to butcher an elk or a deer killed by a car. Lynne and Kathleen do a lot of this kind of work as well. One road kill goes a long way.

Because releasables are developing their hunting techniques, they must be given live food, mice-on-the-hoof. They also need exercise. Volunteers bang on the sides of the cages to urge adolescent raptors off their perches. It is a crude but effective method for getting young birds

Lynne butchers a road kill.

into the air to test and strengthen their wings.

Infant snakes and lizards grow so fast that there is little danger of imprinting. Debbie can hold a garter snake in her hands and drop a goldfish down its throat without having the snake lose its instinct for wildness.

A "first" arrives at the center—a four-week-old female bobcat with one ear chewed off. Fishermen discovered the bobcat floating down a stream, near death from starvation

A visitor at the clinic meets a corn snake.

and a mauling it apparently got from another bobcat. Kathleen's examination reveals infection around the missing ear. The bobcat kitten has maggots.

The little cat will make it, once the infection is treated and she gets food in her empty stomach. She is a beautiful animal with gray, black, and white spots on her coat. Her eyes are midnight blue. On the top edge of her remaining ear is the tuft of hair common in bobcats. Kathleen and Lynne use the heaviest leather gloves, with flaps to the elbows, while handling the bobcat. The loss of an ear and a swollen head do nothing to diminish her willingness to put up a fight. Her claws are small daggers. Kathleen smears salve on the bloody spot where an ear once was. The pitch-smelling ointment makes the bobcat smell of the woods she came from.

The hard part will come when the bobcat is old enough to be set free. Although she is past the age of imprinting, close proximity to people will undermine her tendency to avoid them. She will have to

A bobcat kitten arrives at the clinic.

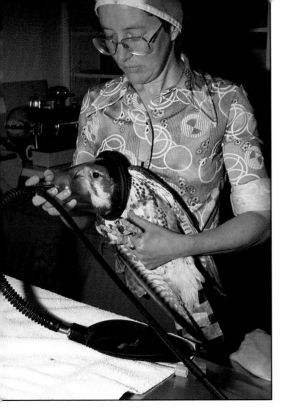

Kathleen anesthetizes a prairie falcon before surgery.

learn to hunt her own wild food. She will require a refuge or preserve where she can gradually adjust to living in the wild again. Kathleen has a network of rehabilitators around the country who help her in such situations.

With baby season in full swing, Kathleen's energy is divided between newcomers and patients that demand long-term care. The great horned owl that was shot in the head is doing well. Kathleen did not believe the bird would make it.

A second great horned owl was electrocuted when it landed on a high-tension wire. The electric charge burned a hole in one foot. The current then traveled through the bird's body and came out at the right shoulder, leaving a hole in the wing. The owl is slowly recovering.

The Cooper's hawk with a leg fracture has developed infection at the point of the break. Kathleen explains to Lynne that she thinks the injury was caused by a sibling in the nest.

An adult Cooper's hawk stands fifteen inches high and has a wing spread of just over two feet. Fast and powerful, these birds need strong legs to capture food in the wild.

Lynne prepares for surgery. A heating pad is placed on the operating table under bright white lights. Next is a towel, and on top of this, the patient.

The hawk looks delicate and out of place on its back under the lights. Lynne covers the bird's head with a clear plastic cone that is linked to the anesthesia machine by a curling tube. The hawk struggles to be free as an anesthetic called Isoflorane passes through the tube to the cone. Isoflorane is an inhalant, the lightest form of anesthetic available. Kathleen uses it on all of her surgical patients.

In seconds the hawk relaxes. Lynne watches closely, measuring the dose of sleep-inducing medicine with great care. The bird's breathing must remain steady, with no gaps.

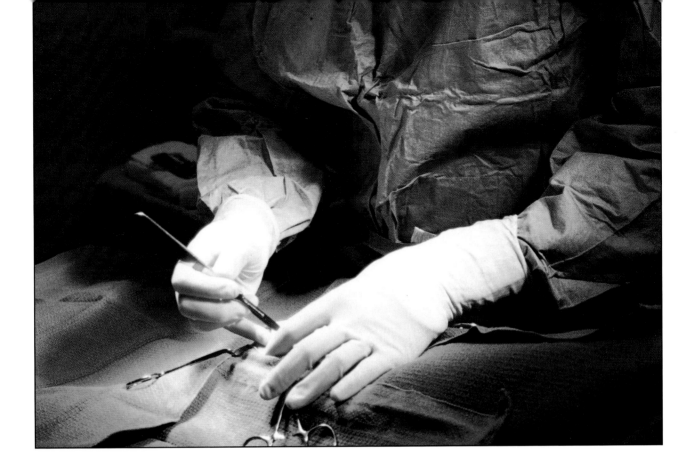

Kathleen goes to work. She bends close over the bird in complete concentration, as if nothing in the world exists except the small exposed area of wound illuminated by brilliant lights and surrounded by sterile cloth. She uses a number 11 scalpel to scrape away infection. A drop or two of blood stains the blade.

The Cooper's hawk rests after surgery.

In previous surgery on the hawk, Kathleen used a steel pin and wires to hold the bones together. But the technique failed. Now she rigs an external cast made with wires and pink denture material. The arrangement looks strange, but Kathleen is convinced it will work. Satisfied with her effort, she tells Lynne to bring the bird back to consciousness.

The hawk comes awake quickly and once more tries to get free. Lynne wraps it in a towel.

"The sign of a successful surgery is a patient that gets up and walks off the table," Kathleen jokes.

If the bird's breathing remains steady, it will go back to its outside cage after an hour.

When the Cooper's hawk surgery is over, Kathleen goes into the reception room. A small girl is waiting. The girl is with her father, a large dark-haired man who looks worried. In the girl's arms is a goose nearly as big as she. The goose is hurt. Kathleen takes the goose and holds it. She smiles at the child.

"It doesn't seem too bad," Kathleen says, doing a quick examination with her hands.

The child, who is about five, seems to be trying not to cry. Kathleen has given her hope. The father explains in a soft voice how the girl's brothers were playing with a new BB gun and managed to shoot the goose. He wonders if its leg might be broken.

Kathleen agrees that the leg is broken but says it can be fixed. The father asks her to go ahead. "Do whatever is necessary," he tells Kathleen.

In thirty minutes the goose has a steel pin in her leg, a cast made of red bandaging material, and a fistful of grain in her belly. After an hour of observation, the goose can go home with the little girl. Her father looks relieved and grateful.

Next comes a turtle hit by a car. It needs head, nose, and mouth surgery. Kathleen tells Lynne it will take the turtle a long time to mend. "Everything turtles do, they do slowly."

It takes a long time to put the turtle to sleep. Turtles and other reptiles shut down their systems under stress.

A clinic volunteer talks with the girl about her goose.

They go into a form of hibernation. A reptile with a metabolism that runs in low gear must be anesthetized with extreme care, or it may be overcome and die.

Lynne knows the inhalant has taken effect when the turtle's bladder empties, a sign that its muscles are relaxed.

"Eventually they lose and I win," Kathleen says, referring to the reptilian response to anesthesia.

The turtle needs reconstruction work on its tongue and on the bony plate at the roof of its mouth. Lynne holds the pointy pink tongue out of the way with a pair of tweezers so that Kathleen can work inside the animal's mouth. She sews a gaping wound shut with thread that is almost too fine to see. The stitches will be absorbed by the turtle and will not have to be removed.

Kathleen has favorite remedies for reducing swelling and encouraging healing. She uses a popular over-the-counter hemorrhoid medicine because it is so effective. The turtle gets a dab before the operation is over. The prognosis is good: the turtle will eventually make it back to the wild.

"Turtles and other reptiles are infinitely slow to heal," Kathleen tells Lynne. "This one will need to be tube-fed for a long time."

The day the turtle is operated on, a fat green toad is delivered to the center. A woman found the toad in her garden. She could see it had been hurt during an encounter with the family cat.

Kathleen examines the toad and discovers a mouth injury. She is not sure how to handle the problem and decides the toad can wait until morning for surgery. She wants to read up on amphibians before putting the animal under the knife.

The next morning Kathleen anesthetizes the toad. Debbie is her assistant. An important muscle called the frenulum has been torn from its moorings. Without surgery, the toad will be unable to eat.

Kathleen sews the muscle in place. She rubs on some *Enserada* salve to promote healing. The toad will recuperate slowly in a terrarium.

During baby season, Kathleen's attention is caught up in the tasks surrounding the care of orphaned animals. Meanwhile, her standard veterinary practice — the treatment of dogs, cats, and pet canaries — goes on. Often Kathleen is faced with an injury or situation she knows nothing about. There are many books on cat, horse, and dog diseases. But there are few on Kathleen's primary interest, birds. Avian medicine is a new and developing science. Kathleen reads, consults other experts, and experiments. One success breeds another. A leap into the unknown leads to deeper understanding the next time. The frontier aspects of her work drive Kathleen forward.

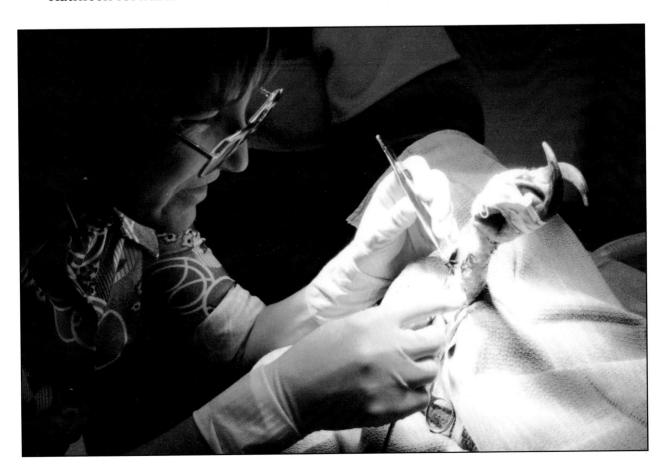

Return to the Wild

PART THREE

The right environment for the release of animals that have depended on humans, or that have been imprinted, is essential. Imprinting does not ruin all chances for freedom, but it makes release more complicated. People who rehabilitate wild animals have learned ways to coax them back to independence.

Kathleen believes that an animal born wild has the right to die that

Kathleen with an elk who will gradually be reintroduced to the wild.

way. She starts planning for release when an animal arrives. Making a sick creature well, or providing a home for the orphan, is only part of what Kathleen must accomplish.

Every baby animal is born knowing about itself. As the animal grows from infant to adult, its senses and skills are fine-tuned by experience. The best way for a young animal to learn is from its elders, a child from its parent. Even a wild animal baby needs clues on how to survive in the wilderness, a knowledge best passed on by one of its own kind.

By summertime the elk at the shelter are six feet tall. The deer almost knock a person down with their affec-

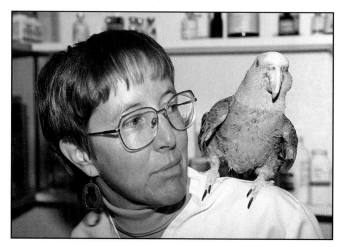

tionate bumps. All of the spring crop of bottle babies are approaching an age when they can be let go.

Kathleen struggles to plan the future for each animal in her care. Imprints need help during their first season of freedom. Special dangers lurk for raptor imprints, for they may seek human company. An eagle might sit on a fence post and watch children play. Unusual or unexpected behavior in raptors is especially misunderstood by people. Sometimes people do not stop and think. They run for their guns and shoot.

Dr. Ramsay's son, Ty, has no fear of these animals that are so much bigger than he is.

Release may mean another form of captivity, a zoo or a living museum where an imprint need not experience a complete lack of human help. More often it means a return to a pure wild state. For many captive animals the return to freedom requires a transition, a time between being dependent and being utterly free.

A young raccoon with an insatiable curiosity is likely to get into trouble without its mother in charge. Mother raccoons supervise their young. They keep them close at hand. In a language of purrs, grunts, chirring, and

screams, a mother raccoon passes information and communicates. The baby listens and watches. A mother's sensitive fingers explore a pool for minnows and tadpoles, or search a river's edge for crayfish. The baby shares a meal when its mother plucks ripe berries from a bush. When danger comes, the youngster scrambles up a tree behind her with arms and legs outstretched.

A wildlife refuge in northern New Mexico, near the Colorado border, will be a new home for the raccoons Kathleen has fed and watched over for weeks. The woman who runs the refuge has agreed to take them into her personal care. Over a period of time she will take them for walks along a stream where crayfish have been deliberately placed. She will "hunt" for the crayfish herself and show the young raccoons how it is done. Eventually the crayfish will no longer be provided, and the raccoons will fend for themselves.

Just as a raccoon parent teaches its young, so does a beaver. In the wild, a beaver mother instructs her kits in beaver ways. The youngsters learn to feed themselves, escape danger, and build dams or tunnels, depending on the stream they live in. Because Wally and

Theo were newborns when they arrived at the center, there is little chance they can be rehabilitated to complete wildness as the raccoons can. A middle ground must be found.

A living museum near the center, a place called Ghost Ranch, is eager to take Wally and Theo. The museum residents are animals native to New Mexico, imprints or creatures too seriously injured to go wild. At Ghost Ranch the beavers will have a large enclosure to live in, and a real stream to play in. Wally and Theo need and enjoy human company. Ghost Ranch is near enough that Kathleen can visit the beavers and take them for walks.

The deer and elk will go to a mountainous region called Brazos Cliffs. Near the cliffs there is a small community of people willing to provide hay and grain through the first winter. By spring the elk and deer will be well on the way to independence. By the second winter they will know how to paw through the snow and find their own forage.

The Brazos Cliffs, with Heron Lake in the foreground.

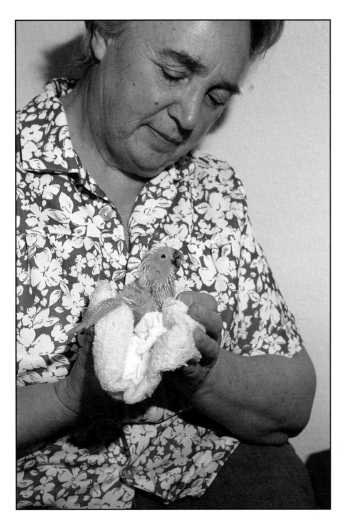

A baby cockatoo comes in for a checkup.

The bobcat is still a question. She is wild and difficult to handle. From the age of four weeks she has been captive and dependent on human care, and she requires a transitional return to wildness. As July ends, no new home has been found for her.

The world does not stand still while Kathleen ponders the best homes for her releasables. Apart from the usual stream of stray cats, kittens, and puppies coming into the center, there are exotic birds.

Some are parrots. Others are macaws and cockatoos. Most have an illness or injury. A few come in because they have been neglected or abused by their owners.

A woefully miserable-looking Amazon parrot comes in, dropped off by someone who does not stay to discuss the bird's condition. The parrot has no feathers; it has pulled out every one. A parrot as bare as the day it was hatched signals neglect. Unhappy birds tend to pluck themselves.

Kathleen keeps a pet African gray parrot in the reception room. The two birds meet. It is love at first glance. The parrots pledge their troth with shrill cries and ear-splitting shrieks. They rub heads and nuzzle, screaming so loudly they have to be moved into a back room.

Kathleen refuses to return the featherless Amazon to its owners.

Birds come in from other rehabilitation programs as well. One is a male golden eagle slated to be the sacred bird for a nearby pueblo called Jemez.

Pueblo Indians worship animals that represent clans, or family groups. The golden eagle is a symbol for the clan at Jemez. An injured bird that cannot go wild is perfect for living at the pueblo and taking part in ceremonials.

In his previous home, the golden was not well treated. A bullet hole in one wing is infected. The bird is dehydrated and suffering from malnutrition. Kathleen tube-feeds the eagle with electrolytes and fluids. She puts salve on the wound and bandages it. It may be months before the bird is healed. When he is, she will give him to Jemez Pueblo, where he might live another twenty-five years.

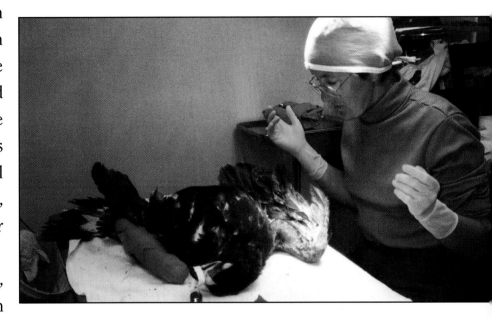

Kathleen works on the golden eagle.

In a quiet moment, Kathleen sits in a chair in her small office and reads a paper she will soon deliver to the American Avian Veterinary Association. The subject is a specialty of hers — distal metacarpal pinning in raptors. The trip to Chicago for the association convention will be her first time away from the center, for more than a day or two, in three years.

Debbie, filling in for Lynne, knocks and comes in. A baby skunk has arrived. The skunk is a few days old, a male weighing thirteen ounces. He was found wandering by the side of the road, his mother probably run over by a car. Because he is still too young to flex the muscles around his scent glands, he is unable to spray.

The skunk will have to be bottle-fed and therefore will be imprinted. When he is old enough to spray, he will still be in human hands. Kathleen must operate and remove the glands.

The skunk is asleep on a heating pad on the operating table. A towel is rolled under his body to prop his rear end in the air. His

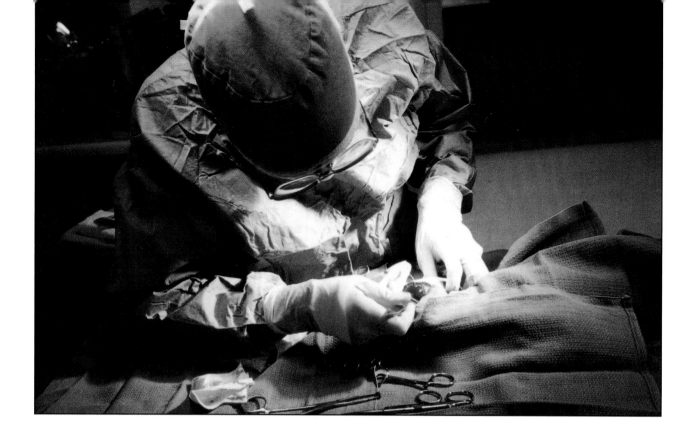

tail is pulled up and pushed back. Debbie keeps track of the anesthesia while Kathleen begins the surgery.

Kathleen cuts a two-inch gash on the right side of the anal opening. She probes with a scalpel and cuts until she finds the gland, a yellow bubblelike object about the size of a grape. She removes the gland and drops it into a plastic bag.

Debbie checks the anesthesia. She introduces more inhalant into the skunk's lungs.

Kathleen works on the left side of the anus, making a second cut and repeating the procedure. Another gland is dropped into the bag. With baby-fine thread she sews the wounds closed and covers them with the same over-the-counter ointment used on the turtle.

Everything has gone perfectly. The glands remain sealed, and there is only the slightest aroma of skunk in the room. Then Debbie gets curious. She pokes one of the glands with a knife. It breaks.

The room quickly fills with a nauseating dose of pure, rank skunk smell. Kathleen and Debbie instinctively rear back to try to escape the odorous cloud.

With one hand clamped over her nose, Kathleen reaches into a cupboard and pulls out a can with a nozzle top. She presses the nozzle and a chemical spurts out, an antidote to skunk odor. In minutes the air begins to clear. Still, it is weeks before people stop commenting on "the skunk incident in the operating room."

Although the little skunk will be defenseless without his scent glands, his future is not grim. Like many others upon whom misfortune has fallen, he will live out his life at Ghost Ranch. He'll be fed every day and admired by visitors, and he'll never have worries about enemies.

Kathleen is dedicated to seeing her patients go free. Nothing can match watching an animal liberated from confinement, bindings and restraints gone, bandages discarded forever. Eighty percent of the animals she treats return to the wild, or a near-normal life.

There are times when surgical skills and sheer determination are not enough.

Barney arrives, an Amazon green parrot with air-sac problems. About twenty-five, he is middle-aged for a parrot and has a chronic sinus infection. A wing was once broken, and he cannot fly. Though his ailments have been let go too long, Kathleen is eager to work with him and try to make him well.

Barney has surgery to correct the air-sac trouble. After a few days, another operation is necessary. The second time around, with Barney

Kathleen struggles unsuccessfully to save the Amazon green parrot.

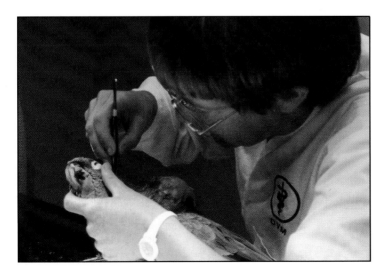

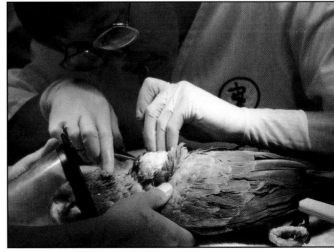

limp on the table under the lights, Kathleen explores and finds avian tuberculosis. Barney has no chance for a good life.

Barney isn't strong enough to survive the second surgery. Kathleen cries at the loss. She is troubled and sad to see him go.

With permission from Barney's owners, his bright feathers are given to the Indians. Parrot feathers are rare in a land where owls and ravens dominate.

Kathleen is consoled by the thought of Barney's gentle spirit living on, visible as a topknot on a child's treasured kachina or as part of a dancer's regalia.

Seasonal changes describe and define Kathleen's days. September brings cold nights and brilliant, sunny afternoons. Fall migration is underway. Ducks fly south. Hawks and eagles also fly south. Kathleen finds a solution for the bobcat.

A rehabilitation program in Oregon suits the young cat's needs. She will be placed in an enclosure about one-third of an acre in size. Live food will be given — rats and mice. The bobcat will have to hunt in order to eat. Except for water, she will receive only the fast-moving rodent prey. Hunger will motivate her.

She will graduate to bigger enclosures and larger prey. In time she will roam a three-acre site and hunt rabbits and squirrels. When she is completely self-reliant, she will be returned to New Mexico and set free in the mountains she came from.

By mid-September, plans are complete for the release of three raptors that have undergone treatment. They will join their fellows migrating south to warmer country. One is a red-tailed hawk, another is a ferruginous hawk, and a third is a bald eagle. Kathleen is especially happy about the eagle, a mature male. It has been at the center for a year recovering from a gunshot wound.

The birds will be released at Kathleen's favorite place, a national wildlife refuge in southern New Mexico called Bosque del Apache.

The word *bosque* describes a woodsy place where trees grow close together and grass is thick between their trunks. By definition, a bosque is near water. In an arid land like New Mexico, a river supports life that would not otherwise exist.

The Rio Grande has flowed south for countless centuries, its banks and shoulders drooping with willow or overgrown with cottonwood groves. At the

Kathleen with the bald eagle.

Bosque del Apache the river divides into side streams, channels, and pools. Grass and trees provide cover for small animals such as skunks, coyotes, and porcupines. Birds nest in the trees. Wide meadows and fields spread away from the river. These open areas are feeding grounds for sandhill cranes, Canada geese, and ducks. The Bosque del Apache is protected. Hunters are not allowed. There is enough room for many animals to live freely.

Kathleen with the ferruginous hawk.

Kathleen, with her husband, Lou, and her son, Ty, drive down to the bosque in the family pickup truck. The releasable birds are in cardboard boxes in the back. Other people drive down, too—volunteers who have cared for the birds for weeks and want to see the release.

The day the birds go free is cold and half-cloudy. Before sunrise the grassy edges of pools and streams are fringed with ice. Steam curls off the water like smoke. Soon after the sun is up, vast flocks of water birds fly into the sky. They are off for a day of feeding in the fields.

Kathleen gazes out the truck window at the gathering light of a new day. Lou is driving. The truck bounces and bumps over rough ground. A small caravan of cars and trucks follows behind.

The Bosque del Apache National Wildlife Refuge, one of Kathleen's favorite places to release wild birds.

The bald eagle is nearly as big as Dr. Ramsay. It takes great strength to control this powerful bird.

"Where are we going?"

The question is from Ty, who sits between his parents. He is tired and grumpy from being awakened early.

"We're going to set some birds free, Ty," his father answers. "They've been in the hospital, and now they're well. We're going to release them."

Ty is almost too young to understand what the words mean, but he knows from his father's tone that something important will happen.

"Do I get to watch?" the child asks, sounding anxious.

"Of course you do," Kathleen tells him. "We will all be there to watch."

A small crowd forms in the wintry field — volunteers from the center and their families, visitors to the refuge, a game warden. A newspaper reporter has come, and with him a cameraman. A local newspaper is doing a story on Kathleen.

The three boxes are unloaded and set in the field. Kathleen lets the red-tail go first. When she releases it, the hawk climbs with ease into the air, eager for flight. The crowd breaks into cheers and whoops of joy.

The ferruginous is next. The most fierce and aggressive of all the species of birds Kathleen treats, this one beats its wings furiously and twists upside down. A volunteer helps Kathleen get the hawk into position, with her hands on its feet and the bird's back pressed against her chest.

Kathleen stands and describes the bird's injury and treatment. Her voice is thin with excitement. Then she lets the hawk go. It flies into a brightening sky, off in the direction of a line of cottonwoods. Another cheer goes up.

The bald eagle is last. The eagle has a wingspan wider than Kathleen is tall.

Two people help her get the bird into her arms and firmly in her grasp. She tells about the bullet wound, and while she speaks the eagle turns his head. He fixes his glittering eyes on Kathleen's face, his beak slightly open.

Kathleen understands the power of the eagle's wildness, and relishes the moment.

She lets the eagle go. He nearly knocks her to the ground as air whirrs through his flight feathers for the first time in a year. His long legs dangle. In a moment he catches the prevailing wind and soars high.

At first the eagle is a colossal presence that dominates the scene. Slowly he is swallowed by the sky—first a distinct bird shape, then a small dark spot, then nothing. He is gone.

Kathleen stands still and watches, her arms loose at her sides, tears streaming down her face. For her this is a moment that has been a long time coming.

Driving back with his mother and father in the truck, Ty delights in describing what he saw in the field. His voice is shrill with excitement. Words tumble over each other as he tells how each bird went free and became a part of the wide blue sky. He goes on until he is tired, and then he asks a question.

"Where are we going, Mommy?"

"We're going home, Ty," Kathleen answers.

"Like the birds? Do you mean the same as the birds?"

"Yes, that's right. We're going home, just like the birds."